DATE DUE

6-17-78	2-19-8	APR 6 1994	
2-5-79	8-1-89	MAY 0 3 1994	
11-9-80	11-19-89		
4-20	12-30-89	DEC 0 4 1996	
9-15-81	5-30-90	MAR 0 4 1990	
2-11-82	10-24-90	JUL 5 1999	
4-3-82	1-18-91	NOV 1 1 1999	
1-29	10-18-91	SEP 0 2000	
6-18-89	DEC 31 199	NOV 2000	
2-28	APR 2 1 1992	MAY 2 6 2004	
4-28-85	AUG 2 8 1992	AUG 0 1 2008	
9-19-85	NOV 1 8 1992		
7-1-86	12-2-92	AG 0 3	
11-16-86	MAR 1 5	2 3 2015	
1-14-87	APR 2 8	6 2	
2-22-87	SEP 2		
	NOV 5 199		
4-21	FEB 17 1994		
7-9-88	MAR 1 6 1994		

HOW THE ROOSTER

SAVED THE DAY

ARNOLD LOBEL

HOW THE ROOSTER SAVED THE DAY

PICTURES BY ANITA LOBEL

GREENWILLOW BOOKS
A DIVISION OF
WILLIAM MORROW & COMPANY, INC.
NEW YORK

LIBRARY OF CONGRESS CATALOGING IN PUBLICATION DATA
LOBEL, ARNOLD.   HOW THE ROOSTER SAVED THE DAY.
SUMMARY: BECAUSE NIGHT PROTECTS HIS IDENTITY, A THIEF TRIES TO PRE-
VENT A CLEVER ROOSTER FROM CROWING UP THE MORNING.
[1.   ROOSTERS—FICTION]   I.   LOBEL, ANITA.   II.   TITLE.
PZ7.L7795HQ   [E]   76-17602   ISBN 0-688-80063-7
ISBN 0-688-84063-7 LIB. BDG.

TO ADAM AND ADRIANNE

Once, long ago, there lived a large and handsome rooster. At the start of each day he would crow to bring up the morning sun.

One dark night a robber crept into the
barn where the rooster was sleeping.

The robber grabbed the rooster by
the throat and said, "Rooster, you
will never bring up the morning
sun again. I am going to kill you.
The world will always be in blackest
night. No one will ever see me as
I run about the countryside, robbing
and plundering."

The rooster, who was brave and clever,
put his ear near to the robber's mouth.
"What are you saying?" asked the rooster.
"I have been swimming around in the
pond and quacking and quacking for so
long, that I have made myself as deaf as
a stone."

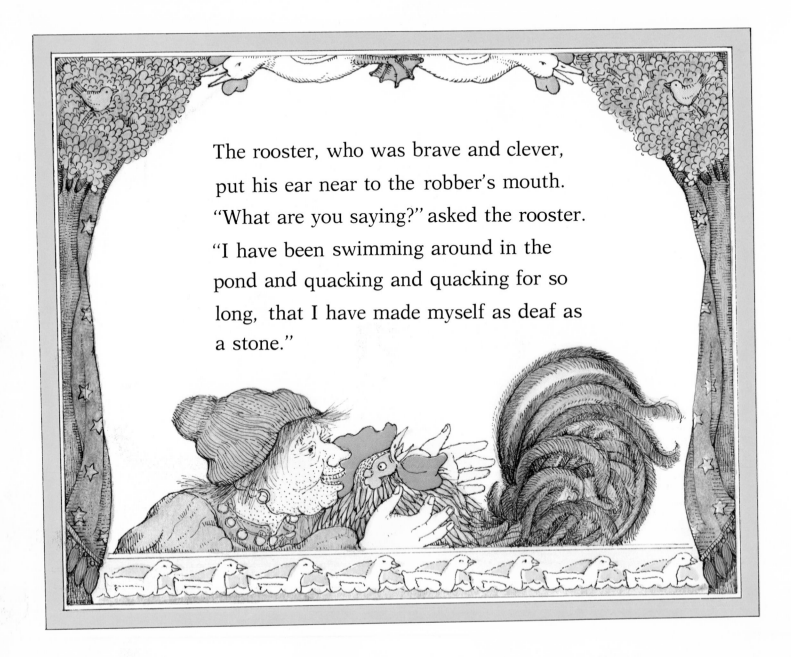

When the robber heard this, he threw back his head and laughed.

"You cannot quack," said the robber.
"It is the ducks who are the quacking ones!"

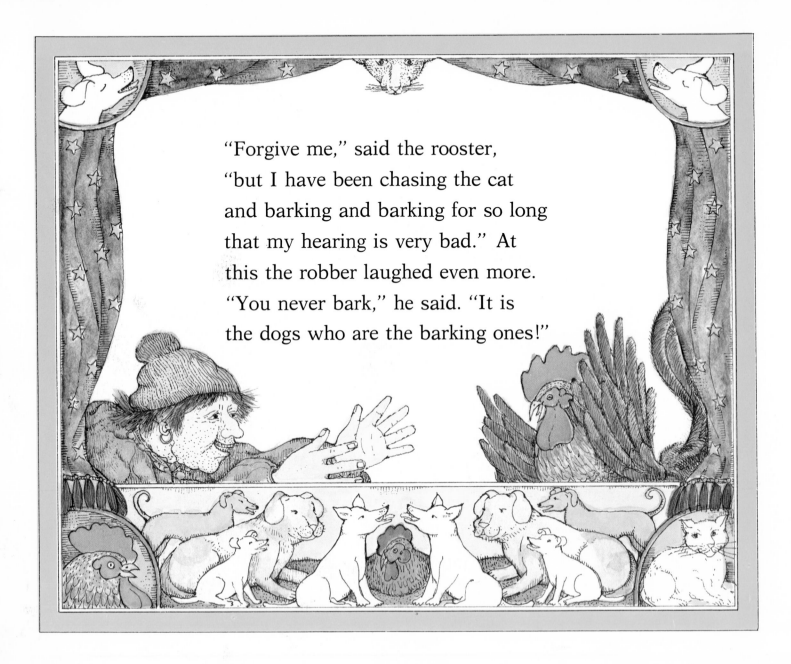

"Forgive me," said the rooster,
"but I have been chasing the cat
and barking and barking for so long
that my hearing is very bad." At
this the robber laughed even more.
"You never bark," he said. "It is
the dogs who are the barking ones!"

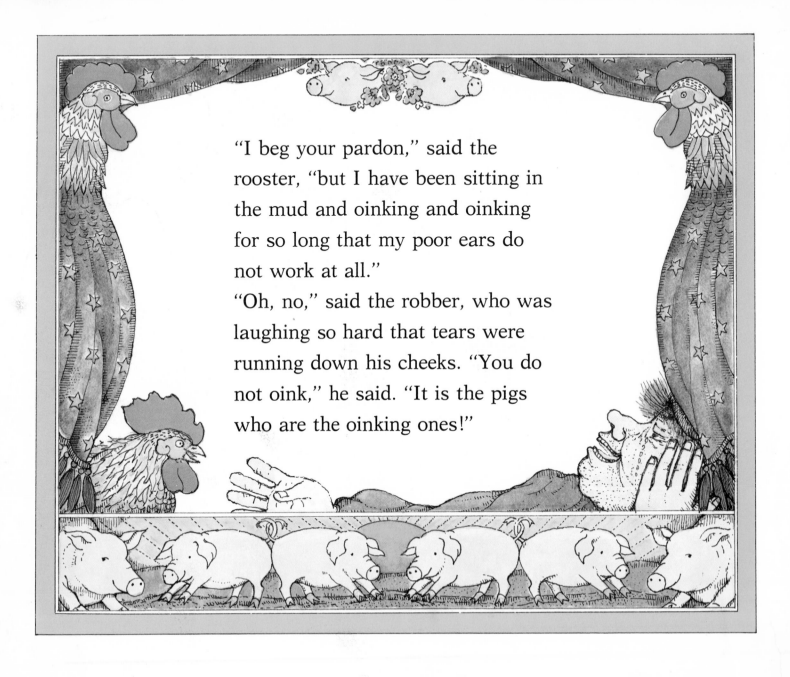

"I beg your pardon," said the rooster, "but I have been sitting in the mud and oinking and oinking for so long that my poor ears do not work at all."

"Oh, no," said the robber, who was laughing so hard that tears were running down his cheeks. "You do not oink," he said. "It is the pigs who are the oinking ones!"

"I am so sorry," said the rooster, "but I have been chewing the grass in the meadow and mooing and mooing for so long that I do not seem to hear anything." The robber fell onto the floor in a fit of laughter. "You foolish bird," he cried. "You cannot moo! It is the cows who are the mooing ones!"

"Enough of this nonsense!" said the robber. "You are a rooster and roosters are the ones who cock-a-doodle-doo!"

"Pardon my old deaf ears," said the rooster. "I did not hear you. Speak a bit louder if you will."

"Cock-a-doodle-doo!" said the robber.
"Please speak up," said the rooster,
"for I am so very deaf."
"COCK-A-DOODLE-DOO!" shouted
the robber as loudly as he could.

The darkness of night faded and
the great yellow sun came up over
the eastern hills.

"You have crowed the sun up for me
and I thank you," said the rooster.
"I have heard you clearly, for my ears
are as sharp as the point of my beak."

The robber, who was well known about the land, was much afraid to be seen by the light of day. He jumped out of the barn and ran away over the fields.

The robber ran far, far away and
the rooster still crows to bring up
the morning sun.